THE CHRISTMAS STORY

Told by JANE WERNER • Pictures by ELOISE WILKIN

A GOLDEN BOOK • NEW YORK
Western Publishing Company, Inc., Racine, Wisconsin 53404

HIS IS MARY, a girl of Galilee.

She lived long years ago, but such a wonderful thing happened to her that we remember and love her still.

One day an angel appeared to Mary.
"You are blessed among women," the angel said,
"for you shall have a son, whom you shall name Jesus.
He shall be called the Son of God, and his kingdom
shall never end."

"I am glad to serve the Lord," said Mary. "May it be as you have said."
Then the angel left her.

Mary married a good man from Nazareth. His name was Joseph, and he was a carpenter by trade.

When Joseph had to go from Nazareth up to
Bethlehem in Judea, to pay his taxes in his father's
town, Mary went with him. It was a long, weary
journey for her.

When they reached Bethlehem at last, they found
many travelers there before them. The streets were full
of cheerful, jostling kinsmen.

The inns were crowded to the doors.
   Though Joseph asked shelter only for his wife,
every innkeeper turned them away.

At last one innkeeper, seeing Mary's weariness and need, showed them to a stable full of warm, sweet hay.

There Mary brought forth her son. And she wrapped
him in swaddling clothes and laid him in the manger,
since there was no room for them in the inn.

HERE WERE IN that same country shepherds in the field, keeping watch over their flocks by night.

An angel of the Lord appeared to them in shining glory, and they were all afraid.

 UT THE ANGEL said to them:

"There is nothing to fear. I come to bring you news of great joy which shall come to all people.

"For a child is born this day in Bethlehem— a Saviour who is Christ the Lord.

"And this shall be a sign to you. You shall find the babe wrapped in swaddling clothes and lying in a manger."

Suddenly the sky was full of angels, praising God and saying, "Glory to God in the highest, and on earth peace, good will toward men."

When the angels disappeared into heaven, the
shepherds said to one another, "Let us go to Bethlehem and
see this thing which the Lord has made known to us."

They hurried to the town and found Mary and
Joseph, and the babe lying in the manger. Afterwards,
the shepherds told everyone they met about the child.

OW WHEN JESUS was still a baby, three wise men from the East came to Jerusalem. "Where is he that is born King of the Jews?" they asked. "For we have seen his star in the East, and are come to worship him."

When Herod the King heard this, he was troubled in his wicked heart. He called the wise men to him and asked them just when the star had appeared.

Then he sent them off to Bethlehem, saying, "Go and search for the young child, and when you have found him, bring word back to me, that I may come and worship him also."

When they had heard the king, the wise men departed. Behold, the star which they had seen in the East went before them, till it stood over the place where the child lay. When they saw the star, the wise men rejoiced and were glad.

And when they came into the house, they saw the young child with Mary his mother, and bowed down and worshiped him. They opened their treasures and laid before him gifts: gold and frankincense and myrrh.

Being warned by God that they should not return
to Herod, they departed for their own country another way.

The child was called Jesus, the name given by the angel before he was born. And the child grew and became strong in spirit and full of wisdom. And the grace of God was upon him.